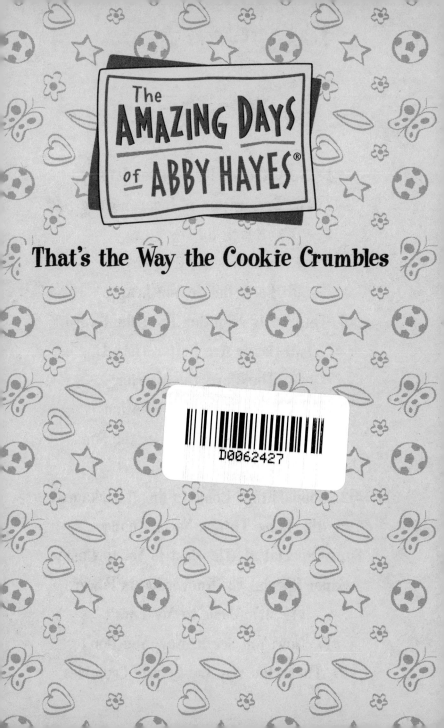

The AMAZING DAYS of ABBY HAYES®

That's the Way the Cookie Crumbles

D0062427

Read more books about me!

The AMAZING DAYS of ABBY HAYES®

That's the Way the Cookie Crumbles

ANNE MAZER

SCHOLASTIC INC.
New York Toronto London Auckland Sydney
Mexico City New Delhi Hong Kong Buenos Aires

ISBN 0-439-68067-0

Text copyright © 2005 by Anne Mazer.
All rights reserved. Published by Scholastic Inc.

SCHOLASTIC, APPLE PAPERBACKS, THE AMAZING DAYS OF ABBY HAYES, and associated logos are trademarks and/or registered trademarks of Scholastic Inc.

12 11 10 9 8 7 6 5 4 3 2   5 6 7 8 9 10/0

Printed in the U.S.A.   40

First printing, November 2005

For Prateeksha, Vinitra, Geerthana,
and Ramyaa

Chapter 1

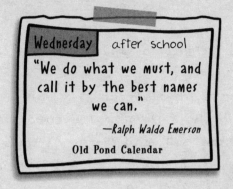

Wednesday | after school

"We do what we must, and
call it by the best names
we can."

—Ralph Waldo Emerson

Old Pond Calendar

What I must do

Bring refreshments for the next meeting of
The Daisy, the middle school literary
journal.

What people usually bring

Peanut butter crackers

Cookies (store-bought)

Fruit

Granola bars

Chips and dip

<u>What I said I'd bring instead</u>
Chocolate chip cookies baked by ME

<u>Why I offered to bring homemade chocolate chip cookies</u>
To impress the staff of <u>The Daisy</u>.

To show them that even a mere sixth-grader has MANY talents. To make them all love and notice me.

<u>How the staff responded to my offer</u>
Fellow editor Lucas practically kissed me. (Thank goodness he didn't!)
He painted a pathetic picture of a starving seventh-grader desperately devouring stale lemon drops from a box. It's been eons since he's eaten home-baked cookies.

Amandine, the art editor, was very impressed. She can't bake at all. She can't get near the kitchen without breaking or spilling something.

Ms. Bean and Ms. Johnson, our editorial advisers, said that they can't wait to taste my cookies!

I acted like I knew what I was doing. But do I?

Abby's Basic Baking Background
I can turn on the oven.
I know where the measuring cups are.
Ditto for the flour and sugar.
I know what a tsp. is.
It's not the same as a TBSP. (Ha!!!)

Other Cooking Experience
Have added water, oil, and eggs to powdered brownie mix.
Have arranged store-bought cookie dough slices on tray and baked in oven.
Have mixed up amazingly disgusting power health shakes in the blender.

AM I OUT OF MY MIND?
How can I possibly do it?

Answers: 1. Yes.
   2. I don't know.

The theme for the first issue of <u>The Daisy</u> is Beginnings.

The theme for these cookies is Beginner.

I COULD buy a mix or frozen cookie dough. I COULD pick up a package of cookies. I COULD say I was too busy with homework to bake.

But I won't go back on my word. I said I would bake chocolate chip cookies from scratch, and I'll do it, no matter what.

I want to make a great impression on <u>The Daisy</u> staff. It's never too late to stun them with my talents. (I hope.)

I can, I will, I must.

And I will "call it by the best names I can."

<u>Best Names</u>

Crazy Chip Cookies?
Daisy Doozies?

Literary Lumps?

It's time to stop talking and to start baking.

P.S. If you can repeat "basic baking background" ten times without stumbling, you win a FREE homemade chocolate chip cookie baked personally for you by Abby Hayes.

P.P.S. Why would you _want_ to repeat "basic baking background" ten times without stumbling? Are you nuts?

P.P.P.S. Speaking of nuts, maybe I should put them in the cookies. Peanuts? Walnuts? Hazelnuts? Almonds?

P.P.P.P.S. My whole family is out at meet-ings, games, practices, and important events tonight. There's no one here to advise me. Or to clean up the mess that I'm going to make. Or to tell me how to avoid mistakes. I'm nuts.

P.P.P.P.P.S. Help? Help! HELP!

Chapter 2

Thursday

"No use crying over spilt milk."

Daily Dairy Delight Calendar

I only spilled a LITTLE milk. And then I wiped it right up. It didn't make me cry at all.

What made me cry was the cookies.

<u>Things That Went Wrong with the Cookies</u>
1. The batter was runny and lumpy. I dribbled it onto the baking sheet and hoped for the best.

2. The cookies were burned at the edges and not baked in the middle. When I tried to scrape them out of the pan, they broke into a million pieces.

3. They tasted funny.

4. I think I forgot something. Maybe it was the sugar.

5. Or did I add too many eggs?

6. The cookies were very salty. They tasted like potato chips, not chocolate chips!!!!!!!

I put the broken, sugarless, over-egged, salty, potato-chip cookies in a container. Someone will eat them, I hope.

A starving squirrel? Malnourished crows? My little brother, Alex?

Then I made another batch. This time I didn't forget the sugar. I measured the salt carefully. I didn't add any extra eggs. We had run out of chocolate chips, so I chopped up some white and dark chocolate bars.

I also threw in nuts and coconut and oatmeal and a bunch of other stuff I found in the cupboard just in case the recipe needed a little extra something. My grandma Emma always puts extra ingredients in her cookies, and they're always delicious.

When I took the cookies out of the oven, they looked fine. I had made more than three dozen large cookies. I let them cool, packaged them up, and put them in my backpack.

After spending four hours assembling, measuring, baking, throwing out, assembling, measuring, mixing, baking again, packaging, cleaning, washing, and scrubbing, I don't care what they taste like. I'm NOT making a third batch.

I promised homemade cookies.
I'm delivering homemade cookies.
Right now that's all that matters.

Abby took a bite of the school lunch turkey special. "I should have gotten the pasta," she said, making a face.

"Beware of the turkey special," her friend Sophia said in a low voice. "Middle School Rule Number Twenty-three."

"I wonder if they'll let me exchange it?" Abby asked. She was only half joking.

"Exchange school lunch?" Sophia repeated. "Um, no, I don't think so."

The two girls were sitting at their favorite table near the window. They ate lunch together every day. Abby's best friend, Hannah, had lunch at a different time.

As usual, Sophia had her sketchbook open in front of her. She picked at her tuna salad and sketched at the same time. Her long dark hair fell over her face.

"I wonder if the mashed potatoes are any better," Abby said. She tasted them and sighed. "Whipped Styrofoam, anyone? My older sisters say the high school food is *much* better. Only three more years to go."

Sophia drew a long curlicue on the page. "We could always bring our lunches in brown paper bags."

"No way! You'll never see *me* carrying a brown paper bag into this cafeteria!"

"I'd decorate mine," Sophia said shyly. "It'd be fun."

"We'd never live it down," Abby said. "*No one* brings their own lunch."

"I guess that's Middle School Rule Number Fifty-one," Sophia said, with a sigh. "I wish I could memorize them all."

Abby pushed her tray away. "Another nutritious but not-so-delicious meal brought to you by the Susan B. Anthony Middle School cafeteria."

"I have a protein bar in my backpack," Sophia offered.

"No, thanks," Abby said. "I baked some cookies for *The Daisy* meeting today. If I'm hungry, I'll have one. I mean, if they aren't too salty or too sweet or too hard or too dry."

"You haven't tasted them yet?" Sophia said in astonishment.

"Ignorance is bliss. I'd rather not know how they turned out until the last minute. What can I do if they're bad, except *feel* bad?"

"I'll try one for you," Sophia offered.

Abby thought for a moment. "Okay," she said finally, "but don't expect too much."

She took the cookie tin out of her backpack, pried open the lid, and removed the plastic wrap that protected the cookies.

"They look fabulous," Sophia breathed. "Like they came from some gourmet store."

"Gourmet? Remember, they were made by *me*." Abby handed Sophia a cookie and closed the tin again.

Sophia held the cookie underneath her nose. She closed her eyes and inhaled deeply.

"Sophia?" Abby said. "What are you doing?"

Her friend blushed. "Nothing like the smell of home-baked cookies," she mumbled. She took a bite of the cookie. Then she took another.

"How is it?" Abby said, frowning. Why wasn't Sophia saying anything?

Sophia ate the cookie slowly without bothering to answer. Then she licked the chocolate from her fingers.

"These cookies are unbelievable," she finally said.

"Unbelievably bad?" Abby asked.

"They're the best thing I've ever eaten in this cafeteria," Sophia pronounced.

"That's because we have the world's worst cafeteria food."

"They're *great*, Abby."

Abby shrugged off the compliment. "So you'd say they're edible at least? *The Daisy* staff won't spit them out in their napkins?"

"If they do, save the rest of the cookies for me," Sophia said. "They're delicious."

"Thanks," Abby said doubtfully. She wondered if Sophia had something wrong with her taste buds.

A few hours later, Abby entered the room that served as headquarters of *The Daisy* editorial staff.

"Abby!" Lucas cried, waving a manuscript at her. His hair seemed to go off in several different directions at once and his glasses were grimy. "Did you bring the cookies?"

Abby nodded. "They're in my backpack."

"Hand them over. Starving mobs of editors are waiting."

"Starving mobs of editors?" Katie repeated. The editor in chief of *The Daisy* was a serious girl with intense dark-brown eyes. She put down her blue pencil and pushed away the stack of papers in front of her. "Speak for yourself, Lucas."

"I am," Lucas said. "I'm dying for those cookies."

"I hope you don't die *from* them," Abby mumbled. They hadn't seemed to harm Sophia, but still . . .

"Cookies? Did I hear cookies?" Matt came rambling over. He was the computer whiz of the group, a tall, lanky boy who wore sandals and shorts even in cold weather.

"Let's have them," Amandine, the art editor, said. She was graceful and calm, with a musical voice.

When Abby uncovered the tin, there was a moment of hushed silence. Then Matt, Lucas, Katie, and Amandine fell upon the cookies.

For a few moments, there was only the sound of chewing. Too nervous to eat a cookie herself, Abby anxiously watched her fellow staff members and waited for their reaction.

Katie was the first to speak. "*Wow*, Abby."

"Are they okay?"

"Fantashtic," Lucas mumbled, his mouth full. "These shouldn't be eaten, they ought to be worshipped."

"Cookie heaven," Amandine said, taking several at once.

Lucas pushed her out of the way. "Save some for me!"

"Don't be greedy," Katie scolded, stepping in front of Lucas to grab her share. "Remember your editor in chief."

"These cookies ought to win an Oscar," Matt said, snatching a huge handful. He leaned back in his chair and stretched out his long, skinny legs. "Or a Newbery and a Caldecott together. Or a Nobel Peace Prize."

"A *Peace* Prize?" Abby said, looking at her friends in amazement. She couldn't believe the way they were gobbling up her cookies. It was almost comical. "For inspiring people to push and shove and stuff their faces?"

"Don't just watch us eat," Katie said suddenly, sliding the tin toward Abby. "Have some. *You* baked them. They're delicious."

"Oh, yeah, right," said Abby. It's about time, she thought. She picked up a cookie and bit into it.

"It's not bad," she said appraisingly. She took another bite and then another. "Hey, these are pretty good." She grabbed another cookie. The tin was practically empty. "Did I make these?" Last night was a blur of chopped chocolate, nuts, butter, flour, and measuring cups.

"Save one or two for Ms. Bean and Ms. Johnson," Katie ordered her fellow staff members. "They'll be here soon."

Lucas looked longingly at the remaining few cookies. "Aren't teachers always on diets?" he asked.

"Don't be a pig, Lucas," Amandine said, reaching

into the tin for another. "Maybe Abby will bake more for us."

"How about for next Tuesday's meeting?" Matt suggested. "Will you do it, Abby?"

"Um, I, uh, I, b-b-but . . ." Abby stammered. Did she really have to do it all over again?

"Don't change the recipe," Katie commanded.

"Um, no, I wouldn't dream of it," Abby mumbled. How could she? She didn't even know what the recipe *was*.

"We'll even chip in for ingredients," Katie added. "Chocolate, nuts, and butter are expensive. Right, staff?"

"Right!" Lucas, Matt, and Amandine all echoed enthusiastically.

Katie threw a couple of dollars down on the table. The other staff members followed.

Abby stared at the money in dismay. "I can't do it," she said. "I mean, sorry, no. It was all an accident. I really don't know how to bake."

"You *do*," Matt insisted. "You can bake better than anyone I know."

"No," Abby protested, but her voice sounded feeble.

"You can be Baker in Chief," Katie said.

"We'll call you Top Cookie," Lucas said.

Of course, Abby had to say yes. But she was mad at herself. All she'd wanted was to impress everyone for five minutes. Did she really want all that extra work?

When Ms. Bean and Ms. Johnson showed up a little later, they didn't notice the cookies at first.

Ms. Johnson handed out stories to edit. Ms. Bean consulted with Amandine and Matt about the layout of the literary magazine.

"You did some capable editing on the last bunch," Ms. Johnson said to Abby, with an approving nod.

Abby blushed. Ms. Johnson didn't hand out praise easily. She was known for her high standards.

Ms. Bean gave her a thumbs-up. "Nice work, Abby."

But then the two teachers tasted her cookies.

"Oh, my," Ms. Johnson said. "These are *amazing*. I need the recipe. Badly."

Ms. Bean's eyes opened wide. "Outstanding. I think these cookies are winners. Abby, what a talent! How do you do it?"

Abby didn't know what to say.

Why did things always happen like this? Why didn't people praise her for the things that *really* mattered? Why didn't they beg her for a poem or a story instead of some silly cookies?

Chapter 3

Sunday

"History repeats itself."

The Crusades Calendar

It better.

Sort of.

I just want the good parts of history.
Not the burned, salty ones.

How DID I make those cookies?

<u>History of a Cookie</u>
1. Disastrous first batch.
2. Clean up and start over.
3. Run out of ingredients, like chocolate chips.

4. Improvise.
5. Add anything you find in cupboard.
6. Get lucky.

Okay, if history repeats itself, I will be prepared.

I'll bake two batches so that I won't get caught off guard.

I'll bake the botched batch tonight. Then I'll bake the better batch for <u>The Daisy</u> tomorrow.

It's a foolproof plan!!!!

"I need the kitchen tonight," Abby announced as the Hayes family sat down at the table on Sunday night. They were having the traditional weekend dinner of roast chicken, potatoes, and salad. "I'm baking cookies."

"*Again?*" her fifteen-year-old sister, Isabel, asked. "Didn't you bake a few days ago?"

"I thought I smelled burned chocolate when I came back from my game last Wednesday," Isabel's twin, Eva, smirked.

"How come you didn't save one for *me?*" their little brother, Alex, said.

"I did, Alex!" Abby protested. "Didn't you see that tin I left in the cupboard?"

"That tin was yours, Abby?" her mother said, raising an eyebrow.

Isabel wasn't as polite. "Those were *cookies*? They were too nasty to eat. I fed them to the birds."

"That explains the poor bloated corpses in the yard," Eva said.

"Shut up," Abby said, without conviction. She hoped that her first batch of cookies hadn't poisoned any innocent creatures.

"Enough teasing," Abby's father said. "Can't we have a single meal without a fight?"

"Dad," Abby said. "Mom. Is it okay if I use the kitchen tonight?"

"Fine with me. I'm planning to watch a movie after dinner," Paul Hayes said, heaping salad on his plate. "Science fiction."

"Ugh." Eva groaned. "Why don't you watch a good sports flick?" Eva was one of the top athletes in her grade.

Isabel wrinkled her nose in disdain. "How about a documentary? Or a classic drama? I bet Dad is watching something revolting like *Attack of the Killer Eyeball* or *Zombie Pinheads from Pluto*."

"Nobody's forcing you two to watch," Paul said mildly to his twin daughters.

"I want to see the killer eyeball movie!" Alex cried.

"It's actually *Attack of the Killer Eyebrow*," Paul Hayes teased, "and *The Zombie Eggplants That Ate Colorado*."

"Cool!" Alex said.

"He's joking, Alex," Eva said witheringly.

"So?" Alex stabbed a large piece of potato with his fork and stuffed it in his mouth.

"Ugh, Alex," Isabel said. "Have you ever heard of table manners?"

"I'm sorry to miss the movies," their mother said to her husband, "but I have paperwork to take care of tonight."

Olivia Hayes was a partner in a busy law firm. When she wasn't working, she served on committees, ran marathons, and read thick books.

"Hey, everyone. Does anyone mind if I bake cookies tonight?" Abby asked again. Her family appeared to have forgotten her.

"Mom, are you *really* sorry to miss a zombie eggplant movie or whatever it is that Dad's watching?" Isabel said incredulously.

With a straight face, Olivia said, "Yes, I am."

Her husband leaned over and hugged her. "The secret of a happy marriage. Don't make fun of your husband's bad taste."

"I need to use the oven," Abby repeated. "Does anyone mind?"

"You have to finish your homework before you watch television, Alex," his mother reminded him.

"I'm only in third grade, Mom," Alex reminded her. "I don't get homework."

"I wish *I* could say that." Eva pushed her plate away. "I have an English paper to write tonight."

"I'm practicing a speech," Isabel added. "Then I have to study for a science test, do five pages of math, finish an art project, memorize a song, and paint my nails."

It was impossible to get through to her family tonight. Did they even hear her talking? Abby drew a deep breath.

"The kitchen," she said loudly. "Going once, going twice . . ."

"I already *said* yes, honey," her father said.

"But Mom didn't," Abby protested. "And neither did Isabel, Eva, or Alex, for that matter."

"If no one protests, that means it's okay," Paul Hayes said.

Abby threw her crumpled napkin on the table. "How am I supposed to know that?"

"Experience," her father said.

"Yeah, but . . ." Abby began. If she hadn't asked, someone would have complained. That was experience, too.

"Is this for Home Technology?" her mother said. "Or a bake sale?"

"Neither," Abby said.

"A party?" Eva asked.

"It's for the next meeting of the literary journal," Abby answered. She couldn't resist bragging a little. "The second batch of cookies I made was so good that the staff begged me to make more."

Her family laughed as if she had told them a good joke.

"Now tell us the real reason," Eva said.

"I already did," Abby said with as much dignity as she could muster.

"They must be some cookies," Olivia Hayes said.

"Yes," Abby said proudly. "They are."

"Save one of the good ones for me, Abby!" Alex said.

"Eva and I want to taste these marvels, too," Isabel said. She began to clear the dishes from the table. "Don't we?"

"Yep," Eva said.

"Sorry, but no," Abby said quickly. That was the trouble with the Hayes family. If you didn't brag, they ignored you. If you bragged, they wanted whatever you had. "I won't have enough."

"It's the least you can do for us, Abby," Eva said. "I mean, you're using the family oven and our household ingredients."

"Abby has a right to use everything in this house," her mother said. "She belongs here, too."

"I'll pay," Abby said. "They gave me money."

"Keep it," Paul said. "We can afford a chocolate chip or two. We just want to taste the results."

"Well, okay. I guess I can save *one* cookie for each of you," Abby said. "But only one. Remember that when you're begging for more."

"Don't exaggerate, Abby," Isabel said. "They aren't *that* good."

"Just you wait and see," Abby said, and scowled. "I'm going to bake the best cookies you've ever tasted."

Chapter 4

Sunday

"Lightning never strikes twice in the same place."

Old Apple Orchard Calendar

Oh, it never does, does it? Well, it struck ME twice in one week. I don't know how I did it, but I baked another good batch of cookies.

Am I lucky, or what?
I've never been lucky before. Not like this.
I keep trying to figure out how it happened, and I can't.

But maybe I shouldn't think about it. Maybe luck is one of those things that can vanish if you look at it too closely.

   Resolution: I will not worry where my luck is coming from.

   Instead, I will put a few cookies on a plate downstairs for my family. They better like them. They better not feed them to the birds.

   The rest of the cookies are in a tin on my closet shelf. They can stay there until the meeting on Tuesday.

   And now it's time for a shower.

Abby wrapped a towel around her freshly shampooed hair and padded barefoot down the hallway. She felt relaxed from her shower. Her homework was done and the cookies were baked. She was looking forward to writing in her journal and then reading in bed until it was time to go to sleep.

As she approached her room, she heard hushed voices and sharp whispers. Abby paused, then tiptoed to the door of her room. She listened for a moment and then pushed it open.

A shocking scene met her eyes.

Isabel was peering under the bed.

Alex was shining a flashlight into her closet.

Their mother was searching in the desk.

"What are you doing?" Abby cried.

Isabel scrambled to her feet. Alex switched off his flashlight.

Olivia slammed a drawer shut and tried to smile at her daughter. "Oh, Abby, I'm glad you're back. We're, uh, looking for, uh . . ."

Abby stared at her family. "Are you searching for my journal?" she asked. "Or a can of purple paint? Or one of my calendars?"

Suddenly, the answer dawned on her. "You're looking for my cookies!"

"We didn't find them," Alex said.

"Shush, Alex!" Isabel said, giving him a dig with her elbow.

"What does the law say about sneaking and entering?" Abby demanded of her lawyer mother.

"I plead the fifth," Olivia said.

"The fifth? This is only the third time I've made them!" Abby cried.

"She's talking about the Fifth Amendment, silly," Isabel corrected her. "It means she has a right to be silent."

"You weren't silent. I heard you all the way down the hall," Abby said.

"Oops," Olivia said, looking guilty. She dusted off her hands and glanced at Isabel for support.

"Do you have a right to go into my room behind my back?" Abby continued. "Is this the kind of thing that Hayes family members do?"

Isabel stepped forward. "It's cruel and unusual punishment to hoard those cookies," she argued. "A family member should not be allowed to torment other family members with the best cookies made in the history of humankind."

Olivia and Alex clapped their hands. "Hear, hear!"

"Those are *MY* cookies," Abby said sternly. "And this is *MY* room."

"But Abby," Isabel pleaded, "the cookies are *so* good."

"That's no excuse —" Abby broke off abruptly. "Did you say 'best cookies made in the history of humankind'?"

Isabel nodded.

"You mean that? *Really?*"

"Of course I do!" Isabel snapped. "Now give us some more!"

"No. You can't have any," Abby said. "You know perfectly well that I'm saving them for the meeting on Tuesday."

"They might be stale by Tuesday," her mother warned. "Use them or lose them."

"Personally, I think it's a tragedy to let cookies go uneaten in their prime," Isabel declared.

"I want to eat them in their tin," Alex said.

"I can put them in the freezer," Olivia offered. "I promise no one will touch them. They'll be safe. And they'll last longer."

"No way! I'm not letting any of *you* within a mile of them," Abby retorted. "And I'm not putting them in the Hayes family freezer without a twenty-four-hour armed guard."

Isabel sighed. "You don't trust your own family. How sad."

"*I* don't sneak into other people's rooms," Abby said. "Not like certain family members that I don't have to name."

"We respect your personal property," Olivia said. "Really, honey."

"We only wanted cookies." That was Alex, sounding pitiful.

"I'll pay," her mother offered.

"*I'll* do your chores for *two* weeks," Isabel said. "And that's my final offer."

Abby pointed to the door. "Out, *now*."

Her mother, brother, and sister slunk shamefacedly out the door.

As the door shut behind them, Abby ran to the closet to check the tin. It was untouched. Breathing a sigh of relief, she sat down at her desk. She opened her journal and picked up her purple pen.

This is getting very weird.

Two Very Weird Things

1. I am capable of baking cookies so good that my normally law-abiding family turns to crime.

2. People are offering me money for them. Even my mother. Even seventh- and eighth-grade staff members of The Daisy.

What's happening here?

Do I have a green thumb for cookie baking? Wait, that doesn't make sense. It sounds like I bake moldy cookies.

I mean — I know what I mean!

Maybe I have a chocolate thumb. Or a

vanilla thumb. Or a walnut thumb. Or a
sugar-and-butter thumb.

I'm getting hungry writing this description.
I want a cookie right now. But I've
promised them to <u>The Daisy</u>. . . .

<u>Two Very Weird Thoughts</u>
1. Wouldn't it be strange if I suddenly
discovered that I'm some sort of baking
genius?
2. What if I could bake fabulous cookies
at any time without much effort at all?

I would become a famous chef and have
my own show on television. And I'd have my
own cookie store, called Lucky Lightning.
People would ask for my autograph on the
street and beg me for my recipes. I'd be a
millionaire. Everyone in my family would
brag about me. They'd all say, "We
thought she'd be the least successful person
in the family, but boy, were we wrong!"
I bet that even my bragging classmate,
Brianna, FOR THE FIRST TIME IN

RECORDED HISTORY, would have nothing to say. For the first time ever, she wouldn't be able to outboast and outbest someone.

My friends Hannah, Sophia, Casey, Mason, and Natalie would celebrate with me.

Simon, on whom I've had a crush since the beginning of sixth grade, would be really impressed. Maybe he'd start inviting me out to the Snowy Owl Café with the other musicians in the Jazz Tones.

Wouldn't it be great if I turned out to be really talented at SOMETHING?

(But do I really want it to be <u>this</u>?)

Chapter 5

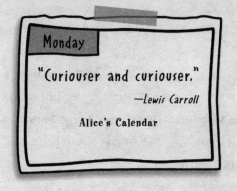

Monday

"Curiouser and curiouser."
—Lewis Carroll

Alice's Calendar

Something VERY curious indeed has happened.

I foiled my family's attempts to get at my cookies.
I didn't eat any myself. (Really!)
I carried them safely to school.
I had every intention of storing them in the school refrigerator until The Daisy meeting tomorrow.

But then, I had to show them off.
At my locker, before lunch, I started to

tell my best friend, Hannah, about the cookies.

She got really excited. "Abby, you are amazing!"

"Who, me?" I said. "Not really. I mean, I don't know why this is happening. It's weird luck or a fluke or something."

"No, it isn't," Hannah insisted.

I didn't answer.

"You have to give me one, Abby," she said. "I can't wait to taste one of your famous cookies!"

"Okay," I agreed. "But just one."

When Hannah saw the cookies, her eyes lit up. I handed her the biggest one. She took a bite.

Hannah isn't shy like Sophia. She doesn't speak in a quiet voice or look down at her hands and mumble.

She jumped up and down and screamed. "Abby! They're fabulous! You're a genius!"

The entire hallway fell silent.

Then, suddenly, as if I had transformed into a gigantic magnet, I was surrounded by kids clamoring for cookies.

I slammed the lid on the tin and made a run for the cafeteria.

Sophia was waiting at our usual table. When she saw the crowd following me, her eyes widened.

I made a detour and tried to duck into the cafeteria line, but the kids wouldn't leave me alone. The crowd got bigger and bigger.

(Now I know how the Pied Piper felt. If only I had a tin whistle instead of a tin full of cookies.)

They begged and pleaded for cookies. They offered favors, like doing my homework or free tickets to school dances.

I refused them all.

Until Simon stepped out of the crowd.

He handed me a dollar and gave me his sweetest smile.

I was powerless before my crush.

In a daze, I opened the tin of cookies and gave him one.

Before I knew what was happening, kids were shoving money into my hand and snatching cookies out of my tin.

In minutes, it was empty.

My pocket was stuffed with dollar bills.

Kids were saying that these were the best cookies they had ever tasted. The ones who hadn't gotten any looked really disappointed. They asked me to bring more tomorrow. But I didn't make any foolish promises.

As soon as I could break free, I stumbled over to Sophia's table and collapsed in a chair across from her.

Without a word, I pointed to the empty tin.

"Why did you let them have all the cookies?" she whispered.

"Because . . ." I said. My voice trailed off. I didn't know what to say. Was it because of my crush on Simon? Or was it the money that convinced me?

Or was it just having something that everyone wanted really, really badly?

When I got home from school and

counted the money, it turned out I had earned a total of forty-five dollars.

Forty-five dollars?
$45.00??
Four ten-dollar bills plus a five?
Or two twenties plus five ones?
A fifty minus five?
Forty-five ones!!!
$45.00!!!!

Yippee! Hooray! Woweee! Zippety-do-dah! Whoop-de-do!!

Of course, now I have to bake again for <u>The Daisy</u> meeting tomorrow. Will I be able to do it? Will my luck hold out?

With so many curious things going on, I wouldn't be surprised at all. And if my luck doesn't hold out, well, then, in the famous words of Queen Marie Antoinette, "Let them eat cake."

"It's kind of fun to do
the impossible."

—*Walt Disney*

Cardboard Box Calendar

I did it. The impossible happened. I baked another best batch. It was kind of fun, mostly. But I'm glad it's over now.

Everyone on <u>The Daisy</u> was thrilled. They wanted me to keep making them, but Ms. Bean said that it wouldn't be fair.

(THANK YOU, Ms. Bean!)

"She's here to be an editor, not a baker," Ms. Bean said. "And besides, we all need to take turns with refreshments. Abby's done more than her share."

Everyone applauded me for making such delicious cookies. I said I would make them again, just not right away. Like, maybe in a year or two.

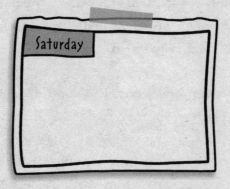

Saturday

What is it with these cookies? As soon as I say I don't want to make them anymore, I'm making them again.

My mother asked me to bake them for her dinner party tonight. She said I could do it instead of cleaning bathrooms this week.
(Does she know that I HATE cleaning bathrooms?)

I baked two batches by doubling the recipe.

*   *   *

Our guests loved them. So did the Hayes family.

My mother said she bought them at a fancy gourmet store called Chip, Chip, Hooray! She winked at me as she said it.

After everyone had left, my family heaped praise on me.

I've never heard my family talk like that to me before. I'm still in shock.

Maybe I _am_ a natural baker. Maybe I _will_ publish my recipes or go to cooking school or all the things they say.

Whatever.

It sounds more exciting than it is.

I mean, I just don't care if I become a billionaire baker or not. In fact, if I don't have to bake for another century or so, I won't complain. I think I'm ready to do something else.

Chapter 6

Wednesday

"Good news travels slowly."

Pony Express Calendar

Does it? I got some really good news to-day, and it only took a minute to travel from Ms. Bean to me.

Before art class, Ms. Bean handed me a brochure.

"I thought you'd like an early look at this," she said. "I'm going to bring it to the next meeting of <u>The Daisy</u>."

The brochure announced a three-week summer program for middle school kids who love to write.

It's at a nearby college. In the morning

there are intensive writing classes. In the afternoon, writers, journalists, and playwrights will give lectures.

This writing camp sounds like it was made for me.

If I attend, maybe I'll find the courage to submit my writing to <u>The Daisy</u>. Maybe I'll become an even better writer than I am a baker.

I need a letter of recommendation, but Ms. Bean has promised to write me one. She said I should get my application in early, as the program fills up fast.

I can't wait to tell my parents.

"I am *so* going to that writing program," Abby said to Hannah as they walked to their next class. She had just finished telling her about it. "My parents *have to* say yes."

"They will," Hannah reassured her. She was dressed, as usual, in bright colors — a cherry T-shirt and orange jeans. Her long hair was braided into a ponytail. "I mean, come on, the camp is educational. Parents love that kind of thing."

"You're right," Abby agreed. "My parents won't even *think* of saying no."

Hannah nodded.

"And besides, Isabel and Eva are going to Europe this summer on an exchange program," Abby continued. "They're touring Spain, Italy, and Greece, then spending four weeks at a language program in France. It's only fair that I get to do a writing camp."

Hannah was about to reply when a girl walked up to them.

"Cookies for sale today?" she asked.

Abby shook her head.

"Did you bring any of those chocolate —" a boy next to them began.

"Nope," Abby interrupted. "Sorry."

"You should start a business." Hannah's eyes sparkled.

"Who, *me*?" Abby said. "You've got to be kidding."

"This is a golden opportunity. Some businesspeople would die for it."

"Come on, Hannah. Can you see me taking orders, delivering hand-wrapped baked goods, and writing out receipts? Besides, I'm done with baking cookies. I mean, *finished*. I'd rather —"

"You could do it!" Hannah interrupted. "You'd earn a ton of money. Maybe you'll even save some for college."

"College?" Abby cried. "We're only in sixth grade!"

"It's never too early," Hannah said. "That's what my mom always says."

"Any cookies today?" Simon asked as he passed the two girls.

Abby blushed deep red. "You liked them?" she said in spite of herself.

"Abby, they were out of this world!" Simon said enthusiastically.

"Uh, yeah, p-p-practically extraterrestrial," Abby stammered.

Hannah tugged on her arm. "Come on, we're going to be late."

"Don't forget me," Simon said. "Save me a few next time you bake." He patted his pocket. "I brought some extra money today just in case."

"I won't," Abby promised. "I mean, I will.

"Why did I say that?" she groaned as Simon disappeared into the crowd of students. "Aaaak!"

Hannah wasn't listening. Her mind was still on their earlier conversation. "It's all set up for you," she argued. "Don't you see, Abby? Customers are begging for your product. It'd be so easy."

"Hannah, *you* should do this, not me."

"I don't bake," Hannah said.

"Neither do I," Abby said. "It's really weird. I mean, how come all of a sudden I start baking great cookies? It doesn't make sense."

"Yes, it does," Hannah insisted. "You just don't know your own talents. But that's what friends are for," she added cheerfully. "I'll help you. We can set it up together."

"Hannah, you're the *greatest*!"

"So you'll do it?"

"No way," Abby said.

Chapter 7

<u>My Dream</u>

To attend writing camp at the college next summer.

Will <u>my</u> dream happen? I hope so!

<u>Dreams of My Fellow Students</u>

To eat my chocolate chip cookies again.

Will <u>their</u> dreams happen? I hope NOT!

There are too many kids thinking about my cookies. They come up to me in the hallways, in the cafeteria, during gym, and even in the bathroom!

Old friends, like Mason, Casey, Bethany, Natalie, and Zach, ask me to make cookies for them.

So do new friends, like Katie, Lucas, Simon, Amandine, and Matt.

Total strangers know my name. All of a sudden, everyone in the school knows who I am and what I do.

Now I know how movie stars feel.
Now I know what it's like to be famous.

Won't anyone leave me alone? Can't I have some privacy?

"And that's the writing program," Abby concluded breathlessly. "Can I go, Mom and Dad? There's nothing else I want to do this summer! Or for the rest of my life!"

"That sounds pretty definite," her father joked.

Abby had gone to their room after dinner to speak to them about the program.

Her parents were getting ready to go to a concert.

Abby's dad was sitting in a comfortable chair while her mother was deciding what to wear. Her favorite dresses were spread out over the bed. Silk scarves were draped over chairs and jewelry was laid out on the pillow.

Abby continued. "Ms. Bean and Ms. Johnson will write recommendations for me. And so will Ms. Bunder, if I ask her."

Her parents didn't say anything, so Abby kept on talking.

"The program is at the college. I can take a bus at our corner right to the campus. You won't even have to drive me."

"Good," her father said.

"There'll be real writers teaching us every morning. We'll also have time to swim or play basketball," Abby said. "It's the *perfect* program. Now that I'm on the literary magazine, I want to develop my writing."

Her parents nodded as if they understood.

Abby also hoped that her older sisters would be envious when they heard that she was attending a college program for the summer.

"It does sound wonderful," her father said.

Abby beamed.

Her mother picked up a necklace and held it up to her throat. "The pink pearls? Or the gold chain?"

"Gold," her husband said.

"I think pearls," Olivia said.

"I think you should wear that dress, Mom," Abby said, pointing to a wool dress with a flared skirt. "You look really good in it."

"Maybe. But what about the blue silk skirt and the matching jacket? I haven't worn them in a long time," Olivia said.

"Whatever you want," her husband said. He checked his watch. "We have twenty minutes."

Abby bounced up and down. "So, I can go, right? The program doesn't cost much, just one thousand, one hundred fifty dollars, plus transportation."

There was a sudden silence in the room. Her parents exchanged a long glance.

"What is it?" Abby demanded. "Don't you think I'm old enough?"

"It's the price tag," her father said. "It's very high."

"We're a bit strapped for cash right now," her mother admitted.

"But Eva and Isabel are going to Europe!" Abby cried.

"It's costing us a fortune. We're overextended," Paul explained. "I don't know if we can afford your writing program on top of everything else."

Olivia glanced at her husband. "Maybe we'll have more money next year," she said.

"Next year is too late!" Abby cried. "My writing career will be *over*!"

Her parents didn't answer.

"Maybe you can sign up for one of the workshops at the public library this summer," Paul suggested.

"The library!" Abby cried indignantly.

"I'm sorry," her mother apologized. "I wish we had a thousand dollars for you."

Her father sighed. "It's a *lot* of money."

Abby stared at her parents. She couldn't believe they were saying no. This was the last thing she expected to hear. After all, her mother was a partner at a law firm. Her father had his own business. Her sisters were going to Europe for the summer. How could they say they were short of money?

"All right," Abby said. Her voice was choked with tears. "Since I can't depend on you, I'll figure this out on my own."

Before her parents could reply, she turned and ran from the room.

Chapter 8

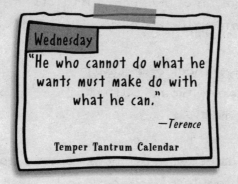

Wednesday

"He who cannot do what he wants must make do with what he can."

—*Terence*

Temper Tantrum Calendar

NO WAY!!

I will NOT "make do" with a public library workshop.

I will attend the writing program of my choice at the college.

All I need is one thousand, two hundred thirty-five dollars or so. (That includes transportation.)

Well, actually six hundred and eighteen dollars.

My parents <u>are</u> going to help me.

Before they left for the concert, my parents came into my room and told me that if I earn half the money, they will find the rest.

Hooray, Mom and Dad!

You came through, after all.

Well, mostly . . .

Half is better than none. I can earn six hundred eighteen dollars, can't I?

I have seventy-nine dollars total. That's more than half the application fee of one hundred fifty dollars. I need to come up with seventy-one dollars right away. Then I'll have a couple of months to earn the rest of the money.

PIECE OF CAKE!!

Or should I say piece of cookie?

Don't Make Do, Make Cookies

1. I'll submit my recipe to a baking contest.
2. I'll win cash for my cookie recipe.

No, it might only be fifty dollars or so.

3. I know! I'll take Hannah's advice and start a business.

4. I'll bake cookies twice a week and bring them to school.

5. What if I bake a double batch of cookies three times a week?

6. Never mind the math. I'll earn tuition money FAST.

7. Are there that many kids who want my cookies?

8. I sure hope so.

9. Disclaimer: If this plan isn't very precise, don't blame me. I'm lousy at math.

10. But I know what the facts add up to: I can do it! I can, I can, I CAN!!!!

If my parents don't have enough dough, I'll make cookie dough instead. (He, he, he.)
I'll attend the summer writing program! I'll become a really confident writer! I'll submit stories and poems to <u>The Daisy</u> that will make the entire school forget about my cookies.

(Wait a minute. They <u>can't</u> forget about my cookies. At least not until I earn the money for my program.)

Hip, hip, hooray!

Chip, Chip, Hooray!

P.S. Must thank Hannah. She gave me the business idea in the first place. Hannah is an idea genius. Will suggest that she start an idea business?

P.P.S. It's funny how things can change so much in a few hours. Just a few hours ago, I never wanted to bake another cookie again. Now I can't wait to start baking.

Maybe it's because I now have "motivation." Ms. Bunder says that's what story characters need. They need to have a reason to do something.

Well, now I have TONS of motivation. I probably have enough for half a dozen characters! Maybe I'll put them in a story this summer.

And now I'm going to call Hannah.

Later

Hannah is going to help me with record keeping, estimating ingredients, and figuring out where to sell.
HOORAY!!!!

With Hannah helping me, how can I fail?

Wednesday night (late)

"Nothing ventured, nothing gained."

Stock Market Calendar

I rummaged in the cupboards and found enough ingredients to bake one more batch of cookies.

When I took the cookies out of the oven, I found myself surrounded by a threatening mob of siblings. I'm NOT kidding!

Alex brandished a laser beam sword.

Eva held a lacrosse stick in her hand.

Isabel carried a dangerous-looking fountain pen.

They looked mean. They looked tough. They looked like they would knock me down.

"What's this, an ambush?" I said.

They moved in on me.

"Give us cookies," they chanted. "Or we'll take them by force."

I placed myself in front of the tray as a human shield and talked fast. "I <u>need</u> these cookies. It's a matter of life and death."

"Prove it," Isabel said.

"I won't be able to attend a writing program if you eat them."

"Do you have some sort of bet going on?" Isabel raised her fountain pen. "You know what Mom and Dad would say about <u>that</u>."

"Yeah, we'll tell on you," Alex chimed in.

"Cough up those cookies," Eva said.

"No more lame excuses," Isabel said.

As my siblings advanced, I looked around desperately. Where were my parents when I needed them? Once again, I had to rely on myself.

"Stop!" I yelled. I tried to look fierce. "If you want to eat them, you pay!"

"That's ridiculous!" Eva said. "We're family."

"Don't you love us?" Alex said.

"Of course I do," I protested. "But I'm selling these cookies to earn money for my summer writing program."

"Mom and Dad will pay for it," Isabel said.

"No, they won't."

My siblings stared at me.

I repeated what my parents had told me earlier that evening. "They're overextended.

They're short on money. They can't foot the bill. The writing program is too expensive."

"But they're sending Eva and me to Europe," Isabel protested.

"That's why they're so strapped for cash," I explained. "It's because of you." I was tempted to stick out my tongue, but I didn't.

"We get to go on a tour of Europe, and you can't do a simple writing program?" Eva cried.

"Dad told me that I'd have my turn someday," I said, enjoying the shocked look on my sisters' faces.

"Poor Abby!" Isabel cried.

"Never mind," I said bravely. "I have a plan. I'm going to bake cookies and earn six hundred eighteen dollars. Mom and Dad will contribute the rest if I can raise half myself."

"Six hundred eighteen dollars?" Eva gasped. "That's a _lot_ of cookies to bake!"

Isabel looked teary-eyed. "Why didn't you tell us in the first place?"

"We're so sorry we tried to steal your cookies, Abby," Eva said.

Alex made a fist. "We'll defend them to the death!"

Then all three left the kitchen. A few minutes later, they came back and handed me ten dollars.

"This is for three cookies," Eva said. "Keep the change."

Thoughts

It's nice that my cookie-stealing siblings gave me ten dollars for a few cookies.

It's nice that they've promised to leave my cookies alone.

But it's <u>not</u> nice that I have to suffer while they get an all-expenses-paid trip to Europe!!!!

Is it because Eva and Isabel were born first? Or is it because their trip was planned first?

Why do I have to work when they don't? Why do I have to worry about money when they have it all?

No matter what Mom and Dad say, it's really <u>not</u> fair!

Chapter 9

Saturday

"Let the chips fall where they may."

Woodcutter's Calendar

The chips are falling into bowls of batter like chocolate rain. The chips are being stirred, spooned, shaped, and baked by the thousands.

When I close my eyes at night, I see chocolate chips. I see cookies in my dreams. And eager hands reaching for them.

I'M ALL CHIPPED OUT!!!!!!

AAAAAAAAAAAHHHHHHHHHHHHHH!!!!!

I haven't had a chance to write in my journal for ages. Every single night I've been baking Abby's Chippy Chocolate Cookies.

Well, <u>almost</u> every single night. Some nights I have to do homework. Or let someone else use the kitchen.

I've also been shopping every single week-end. Hannah helped me figure out how much I needed. Mom and Dad helped me pay for ingredients. We went to a bulk food store to save money.

We bought gigantic sacks of flour, sugar, and chocolate chips. We bought pounds of butter and walnuts. We bought bags of coconut, oats, and some other stuff, like butterscotch chips. We bought huge bottles of vanilla extract.

Dad grumbled that we needed a special storage shed to hold everything. But I promised to make room in our cupboards.

And I did, sort of.

I only had to hide a few bags of stuff behind the couch. So far, no one's found them.

Hannah also helped me make a record book.

She said I should mark down how many cookies I made, how many I sold, any

expenses I had, and how much profit I made. It's called bookkeeping.

I tried it for two whole days.

UGH!

Now I simply bake the cookies, take them to school, and sell them. Then I stuff the money in my jeans pocket, shove it in a drawer at home, and at the end of the week, put the money in the bank.

That's good enough for me.

When Abby reached her usual spot in the cafeteria on Monday at noon, there was a line waiting for her. She found a chair, opened a tin of cookies, and said, "Okay, who's first?"

"Me," Simon said, holding out a pile of dollar bills. "I want six today."

"Only the best for *you*, Simon," Abby said boldly, hoping that she wasn't blushing again. "Are they all for you?"

"I'm bringing them to the Jazz Tones rehearsal this

afternoon," Simon said, putting the cookies in a paper bag.

"Say hi to everyone from me," Abby said. "If they remember who I am."

Once Abby had worked as the assistant to David, the director of the Jazz Tones. But she had quit to join the literary journal.

"They haven't forgotten you," Simon said with a smile. "How could they?" He walked back to the group of seventh-graders who were waiting for him.

Abby's heart was beating fast. That smile — it melted something inside her. Like the sun on snow. Or . . .

"Isn't he *adorable*?" Mason said sarcastically.

"Shut up, Mason," Abby said. "Simon is a very nice person."

"Give me one of your best," Mason mimicked. "I broke my piggy bank last night so I could buy one of your very nice cookies."

Abby rolled her eyes. "You'd better not give me pennies."

Mason handed her a dollar bill. "Let me know if you need help selling," he offered. "I work for free. No payment required — not even a cookie."

"Can I believe my ears?" Abby said. "Thanks anyway, but Hannah's helping me. She's selling them, too, on her lunch hour."

"This is big business!" Mason exclaimed.

"Excuse me, but there are people waiting here," an impatient voice interrupted.

With a mock bow, Mason stepped back. "Madam," he said. "Or is it mademoiselle?"

"How many calories in each cookie?" Brianna demanded, ignoring Mason. The sixth grade's most popular girl was dressed in a scoop-necked pink sweater and boot-cut pink jeans. Her glossy black hair swung over her shoulders. "I have to watch my weight, you know. Actresses always do."

"I don't know anything about calories," Abby said. "How many cookies do you want?"

"One. Make it a tiny one. Do I get a discount?"

Abby shook her head.

"One day you'll brag that I bought cookies from you," Brianna said, giving Abby a brand-new dollar bill and picking up the biggest cookie in the tin. She walked away, nibbling at its edges.

One of Abby's former best friends, Natalie, snorted in disgust. "Sure, Brianna, take the 'tiniest' one." She plunked down a dollar and grabbed the first cookie she saw. "She's got it all wrong, anyway.

One day Brianna is going to brag about knowing *us*."

"You know Brianna," Abby said. "She's in-, in-, what do you call it?"

"Incorrigible," Natalie supplied.

"That's the word," Abby said. "I wonder if my sister Isabel knows it."

Natalie shrugged. "Probably." She turned away.

Once Natalie would have stayed to chat, but now she and Abby rarely spoke. Since starting middle school, Natalie had changed a lot. But it was not only that. Abby had discovered one of Natalie's secrets. Now Natalie didn't like being around Abby very much.

Abby had to admit that she had changed, too, although she hadn't become ultracool and distant like Natalie.

Could she ever have imagined that she'd be selling hundreds of cookies every day, at lunchtime? And that she'd even be enjoying it, just a little?

As Abby sold the last cookie and the crowd of kids vanished, the teacher on cafeteria duty came up to her.

"Sorry, they're all gone," Abby said. "I'll save one for you next time, if you want."

"No, I'm not here for a cookie," the teacher said. "I need to speak to you. Can you come with me for a moment?"

"Of course," Abby said, wondering what the teacher wanted to talk to her about. Maybe the teachers wanted her to bake for faculty meetings or lunch hours? She and Hannah had spoken about expanding their cookie sales to the teachers' lounge.

"In here," the teacher said, indicating an empty classroom. She sat down at a desk and motioned to Abby to take a seat across from her. Then she took a deep breath. "I'm afraid that you have to stop selling cookies in the cafeteria."

"How come?" Abby said, before she could stop herself. She wasn't used to challenging teachers. But was she supposed to shut down her cookie enterprise just because a teacher said so?

"It's against the rules."

Abby's face got hot. "Um, uh, which ones?"

"The ones in your student handbook that forbid selling on school property."

"Sorry," Abby said. "I didn't know."

"That's not an excuse," the teacher said sternly. "At the beginning of the year every new student signed a paper agreeing to the rules in the handbook.

Your parents signed it, too. Do you remember? We have the signed paper on file in the main office."

"Oh, yeah," Abby mumbled. She remembered a few of the rules, like no fighting, no stealing, and no cheating. Those were obvious. And then there were the ones about clothes and swearing. But she didn't remember the rule against selling.

"This has gone on too long. You can't sell the cookies anymore. It's setting the wrong example for the rest of the school. If we allow one person to break the rules, anyone can. What will someone decide to sell next? Games, books, pencils, toys, clothes — you name it."

"Oh," Abby said, imagining a line of vendors in the cafeteria selling pink bubble gum, striped socks, headbands, and water pistols.

The teacher's voice softened. "We would have clamped down on you sooner," she continued, "but the teachers knew you were trying to earn money for your summer writing program. Ms. Bean told us about it. We turned a blind eye as long as we could."

"You mean, you knew I was breaking the rules and you *let* me continue?" Abby said in astonishment.

The teacher nodded. "But now the principal has

heard, and he doesn't like it. We're all going to get in trouble if this continues one more day."

"Wow," Abby stammered. "Thanks."

"Don't let me or any of the other teachers catch you selling cookies in the cafeteria again," she warned. "Or we'll have to send you to the office."

"I won't," Abby promised.

"Good." The teacher looked relieved. "You know, everyone says the cookies are fantastic."

Chapter 10

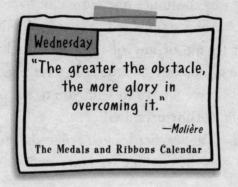

Wednesday

"The greater the obstacle,
the more glory in
overcoming it."

—Molière

The Medals and Ribbons Calendar

My greatest obstacle is the ridiculous, unfair, and terrible rule against selling cookies
in the school cafeteria.

HOW do I overcome this obstacle???

Note: I don't want any glory from overcoming it. I just want the profits!!!

Hannah says that I need to find another place to sell them. Like the Snowy
Owl Café, where the Jazz Tones meet for
hot chocolate.

But I don't want to start a real business. I don't want to bake regularly. I
don't want to split profits with a store. I
only want to bake until I make the money
I need for the writing program.

Facts

1. All my customers are at school.
2. In school, the cookies sell them-
selves.
3. The best way for me to earn money
quickly and easily is to continue selling
my cookies in, around, or near the
school.

Hannah thinks this is dangerous. She in-
sists that there has to be another place to
sell them.
But she hasn't convinced me.

I say that it's too much work, time, and
energy to start all over again. How long
will it take me to find another large group
of people who desperately want to buy my
cookies?

There's only one possible solution.

Somehow I have to find a way around the rules.

"Abby, this really isn't a good idea," Hannah said with a worried frown as the two girls entered the school yard.

"The teacher said no selling in the school cafeteria. She didn't say anything about the *school yard*." Abby pointed to the tins tucked under her right arm. "I have dozens of cookies here, and I'm going to sell them."

Hannah shook her head.

"Don't worry. I'll be careful."

"*Careful?!*" Hannah cried. "You're breaking the rules!"

"Not really. Anyway, who's to know? I won't sell in the same place twice." Abby stopped and scanned the school yard. She saw a bench under a tree at the far end. "That looks like a good spot. Nice and isolated."

"Abby, you're crazy!"

"I have to do it," Abby said stubbornly.

Hannah shook her head. "Count me out," she said.

"Well, okay, then," Abby said, feeling hurt. "I'll sell them without you."

"Come on, I'm still your friend," Hannah pleaded. "I just don't want you to make a serious mistake."

Abby managed a smile. "I'm not making a mistake," she said. "Really. I've thought about it a lot. If I can get away with selling in the school yard for only a few weeks, I'll have almost all the money I need." She saw Mason across the yard and waved.

Hannah sighed deeply.

The two friends said an awkward good-bye. Abby hurried toward Mason. He had offered to help a few days ago. If Hannah wouldn't help her anymore, maybe Mason would.

She felt bad about leaving her best friend behind, but nothing was going to stop her from reaching her goal.

"We have to watch for teachers," Abby said to Mason. "This might be against the rules."

"What dumb rules," Mason said. "They shouldn't squash free enterprise like that."

"Yeah," Abby agreed, glad that Mason understood. It was a relief not to have to argue or explain or defend herself. "I mean, it *might* be okay to sell in the school yard, but I don't know for sure."

"Don't worry. I'll let everyone know that you're here," Mason said. "Everyone except the teachers, of course! We'll have those cookies sold in no time."

Abby stood nervously by the bench and waited as Mason went from group to group of middle school students. There were shouts of laughter and eager looks in her direction.

Soon kids were heading her way. In ten short minutes, the cookies were gone. No teachers or principal appeared to stop her.

Twice a week, Abby sold cookies before school. The word got around. The cookies sold out quickly. Even though she never stood in the same spot twice, kids always found her.

"It's strange to keep shifting places like this," she said one Monday morning to Mason. "It makes me feel . . . well, *shifty*. Like I'm a spy or something. Or a criminal."

"Instead of calling you the Big Cheese, we'll call you the Big Chip," Mason joked. "The boss of the infamous international cookie ring."

"Ha!" Abby said. "So who are *you*?"

"I'm your loyal bodyguard," Mason said.

Abby handed him a cookie. "Your reward, sir." She always baked an extra few for Mason now. He showed up every morning to help her.

Then she plunked herself down on a bench. The first kids were starting to line up. She opened a tin and set herself up for business.

As the cookies vanished, she turned to Mason. "They go so fast. It's practically magic."

"Get your Chippy Chocolates," Mason called. "Straight from the Big Chip herself. Only a dollar apiece."

Two kids stepped up, dollar bills in hand.

A shadow fell across the bench. Abby glanced up and met the gaze of Dr. Trane, the school principal.

"Young lady, hand over those cookies."

"Hey, wait a minute," Mason protested. "You can't do that. Those are hers. She made them herself."

Abby held on to the tin. "What's the problem, Dr. Trane?" she said. "I thought it was okay to sell cookies outside the school."

Was that a lie or was it the truth? No one had tried

to stop her since she'd been in the school yard. Abby had *almost* convinced herself that she wasn't breaking any rules.

"Yeah," Mason chimed in. "She's not doing anything wrong."

Dr. Trane glared at them. "You're both coming to the office with me," he said to Abby and Mason. "March."

Chapter 11

Monday

"That's the way the cookie crumbles."

Spilt Milk Calendar

Is it?

Dr. Trane ushered me and Mason into the main office. I kept telling him that Mason had nothing to do with the cookies, but Dr. Trane ignored me.

He told us to wait outside his office until he was ready. We sat down on two chairs across from the secretaries' desks.

It was embarrassing to sit in the principal's office. The secretaries kept looking at us, wondering what crimes we had commit-

ted. Maybe they thought we'd stolen someone's lunch money, or beat up some de-
fenseless kid, or talked back to a teacher.

I wanted to stand up and shout, "I
only baked some innocent cookies!"

I kept reliving the moment when Dr.
Trane's shadow had fallen across the bench
and he had marched us into his office.

I wondered who had seen me. Brianna,
the most popular girl in the school?

Maybe she was bragging to her friends
about how she never got into trouble, but
she had seen Abby Hayes ushered into the
principal's office right now.

Or maybe Hannah had seen me and was
preparing to say, "I told you so! You
should have listened to me!"

Or Ms. Bean and Ms. Johnson. Could
I get thrown off the literary journal for
this?

What if Simon found out? What would
he think?

Only bad kids got sent to the principal's

office. I had never been sent to the principal's office before. Was I a bad kid
now?

To take my mind off my doom, I stared
at the posters on the wall. They portrayed
hot-air balloons, sailboats, and sunsets, and
had inspiring messages, like, Believe in Yourself, Don't Ever Give Up, and Go After
Your Dreams.

Yeah, right. What got me into so much
trouble in the first place?

I had gotten Mason into trouble, too. I
felt awful about that.

But Mason wasn't mad at me. He was
mad at Dr. Trane.

"Dr. Trane can't take your cookies," he
fumed. "He <u>has</u> to return that tin to you.
Or pay you what it's worth. It's your personal property."

"Maybe," I said doubtfully. I wasn't
that worried about the tin. I could always
make more cookies. I was much more
scared of Dr. Trane.

After ten minutes, Dr. Trane called us into his office. We sat down in front of his desk. There were more inspirational posters on the wall and more uplifting sayings.

But I didn't feel inspired or uplifted as Dr. Trane cleared his throat and frowned at us.

"I'm going to read you the riot act," he finally said.

"Since when do cookies start riots?" Mason said.

Dr. Trane didn't think that was funny. "You've both read the Student Handbook, I believe." He picked up a couple of sheets of paper and waved them at us. I saw my signature and my mother's. "As you know, there's a strict rule against selling on school property."

"She wasn't bothering anyone," Mason muttered.

Dr. Trane looked directly at me. "You were recently warned to stop selling cookies. So why did you keep doing it?"

"Um, uh," I said, "I, uh, I thought it meant, uh, inside the school. I, um, thought it was okay to sell outside."

"How could you think that?" Dr. Trane demanded.

I couldn't say anything.

"You willfully and knowingly ignored school rules," Dr. Trane said. "This is going to have consequences. This is not acceptable behavior."

"Mason was just an innocent bystander," I pleaded. "I was the one selling the cookies. Could you send him back to homeroom, at least?"

Mason jabbed me in the ribs. "Shut up," he mumbled.

"You're both on lunch detention this week," Dr. Trane said sternly. "You'll report to my office at lunchtime starting today. If I see either of you selling <u>anything</u> again, you'll be suspended. This is a final warning."

I was shaking. Even Mason looked a little pale. Then he dismissed us.

"Uh, Dr. Trane – um, may I please, uh, have my tin back?" I said. "I'll just take it home."

"I'm confiscating it," Dr. Trane said. "It's school property now. You can pick it up at the end of the month."

"But . . ." I protested.

"That's a tragic waste of cookies," Mason said.

"You're both lucky not to have worse consequences. I'm in a good mood today," the principal said. "Now get out of here before I change my mind. And don't let me <u>ever</u> see you selling cookies again on school property."

Mason and I stumbled out of the office.

"I'd hate to meet him in a dark alley when he's in a <u>bad</u> mood," Mason said.

"Yeah," I said gloomily. "I'm not looking forward to lunch detention."

"It could be worse." Mason tried to cheer me up. "He might have called our parents."

"I guess," I said. My legs felt wobbly at the thought of it. My parents knew I was selling cookies, but I had never told them what happened in the cafeteria.

And what would my lawyer mother say about the paper she and I had signed at the beginning of the year? The one saying that we understood and promised to obey all school rules? I didn't want to know.

"Hey, Mason, I'm really sorry about this. . . ." I began.

"Ssshh," he said.

"But I got you into trouble."

"So what?" He changed the subject. "I wonder if we can rescue those cookies. We can sneak into Dr. Trane's office, take the cookies, and leave him the tin. Call it Operation Cookie Grab. He'll never know the difference."

"Don't even <u>think</u> about it," I said.

Scary Thoughts

I deliberately flouted the rules.

I lied to Dr. Trane and my parents and got Mason into trouble.

I almost got suspended from school.

I have lunch detention for a week.

Will this go on my permanent record?

Will the writing program reject me if they find out?

Help!!! WHAT HAVE THESE COOKIES TURNED ME INTO?

Soothing Thoughts

I'll probably find another place to sell the cookies.

(But I can't ask Hannah for help again, because then I'd have to tell her what happened, and then she'd say . . . Wait! That's NOT a soothing thought!)

I'm only a hundred fifty dollars short for my writing program.

I didn't get suspended from school.

My family doesn't know I got in trouble.

Silly Thoughts

I wonder if Dr. Trane will eat all the cookies.

Or will he share them with the other teachers?

Will they just lie forgotten in their
tin?

Sad Thoughts

This is the first time I've ever been in
trouble!

It feels even worse than I imagined.

Nobody else can find out!

Chapter 12

Tuesday evening

"Appetite comes
with eating."

Gobbling Gourmet Calendar

I haven't had any appetite yet this
week. It's impossible. Who could eat under
the cold eye of Dr. Trane?

<u>Lunch Detention in the Principal's Office</u>
There's just me, Mason, and one other
boy, a pimply, nerdy eighth-grader. I can't
figure out what he did. He doesn't <u>look</u>
like a troublemaker. But I don't,
either.

Maybe he hacked into the school's computer system and changed all the grades?

Mason and the pimply kid devour their

food. I pick at mine. In Dr. Trane's office, the school lunch tastes worse than usual. Is that possible?

Dr. Trane doesn't say much. He reads files (ours?) and makes notes (on us?). He clears his throat a lot.

If Mason and I so much as look at each other, Dr. Trane says, "Quiet!"

No one dares to say a word.

When lunch period is finally over, I sneak out, hoping that no one sees me leave the principal's office.

The secretaries shake their heads. Maybe they're thinking, There go the school criminals, the cookie baron and her bodyguard and the evil computer whiz.

Or maybe they're thinking something like, What a shame these kids have to eat with Dr. Trane! He'd make us lose our appetites, too!

"Wednesday lunch, under the evil eye of Dr. Trane," Abby wrote on a napkin. She passed the napkin under the table to Mason. "Day number three. The juvenile delinquents eat their spaghetti."

Mason tried to suppress a smile. But not quickly enough.

"What's going on?" Dr. Trane demanded.

"Nothing," Mason said. He crumpled up the napkin and wiped his hands on it for good measure. "We're eating our delicious school lunch."

Abby shoved a forkful of spaghetti into her mouth. There was nothing worse than cold, slippery school spaghetti.

The pimply kid slurped his chocolate milk.

"You have two more days," Dr. Trane said. "Unless you've enjoyed my company so much that you'd like another week."

"Oh, no, thanks," Mason said, burping.

The principal gave him a warning look and returned to his paperwork.

Abby didn't dare look at Mason again. The pimply kid scratched his nose.

The secretary knocked at the door. "Dr. Trane? There's a parent here to see you. Can you come out for a minute?"

Dr. Trane stood up. "Finish your lunch *quietly*," he said to Abby, Mason, and the eighth-grader. "I'll be back. Woe to you if I find you talking."

As the door closed behind him, Abby and Mason

turned to each other. The pimply kid pushed his tray away.

"Woe to you!" Mason repeated gleefully. "Woe to you and you and you . . ."

"Ssshhh!" Abby interrupted. "He might come back."

"Who cares, anyway?" the pimply kid said. "The worst he can do is give us another week of detention."

"Another *week*?" Abby repeated. "I don't think I could stand it."

Abby shuddered to think of the excuses she'd have to make. She had already lied to Sophia. She had pretended that she was doing a project for the literary journal during lunch hour this week. Hannah, fortunately, had a different lunch hour than Abby and Sophia. Abby hadn't lied to Hannah, unless you counted not telling her at all. Abby had also lied to all the kids who asked her for cookies. She told them that the family oven was broken.

But she couldn't keep this up much longer. It was just a matter of time before someone figured out what was happening.

Mason leaned back in his chair. "I wish I could buy a soda."

"If you give me two dollars, I'll climb out the window and get one for you," the kid offered.

Mason emptied his pockets, pulling out a dollar, three quarters, and a couple of nickels.

"Are you both out of your *minds*?" Abby said.

"I have a dollar eighty-five," Mason said.

"I won't take less than two dollars," the kid said.

"Come on, I'm only a few cents short," Mason begged.

The kid folded his arms across his chest. "It's too much of a risk."

"Cheapskate," Mason muttered.

"You're short fifteen cents," Abby said. "I'm short one hundred and fifty dollars."

"What are you in for?" the pimply kid asked her. "Stealing?"

"Selling cookies," Abby said.

The kid's eyes lit up. "You mean the Chippy Chocolate Cookies? *You're* the cookie kid?"

Abby nodded.

"Those cookies are awesome. Worth stealing, if you ask me."

"I *didn't* steal them," Abby said. "I made them."

"Dr. Trane confiscated a whole tin of cookies,"

Mason said. "They're hidden in this office somewhere."

"Let's search for them!" the kid said.

"No, absolutely *not*!" Abby cried, forgetting to talk quietly. She clapped her hand over her mouth.

"Why should Choo-Choo Trane get to eat them?" the kid said.

"We can't search his office!" Abby hissed. "If he found us, we'd get detention until *college*!"

The door swung open. Abby froze as Dr. Trane poked his head in the room.

He frowned at the three students. "Did I hear talking?"

No one said anything.

"Good," Dr. Trane said. "Keep it like this." He shut the door.

Everyone breathed a sigh of relief.

The pimply kid looked at the clock. "Only ten more minutes of this stupid detention," he complained. "At least for today."

"*Sshhh!*" Abby said.

"It's dumb," the kid repeated more loudly. "Dumb, dumb, dumb."

"Shut up," Mason said. "You'll get us all into trouble."

"So?" the kid said.

"I think I hear him again," Abby whispered.

"Dumb," the kid muttered one last time.

The door opened again. Abby held her breath, Mason pretended to eat, and the kid picked at his teeth.

Dr. Trane hurried into the room. "You're dismissed," he said. "I'll see you tomorrow."

Abby swung into the hallway, with Mason close behind her. "That was close," he said. "That kid almost blew it for us."

"What is it with him, anyway? Does he enjoy detention?" Abby asked. "I hate it! I never want to be in detention again!"

"Me, neither," Mason said. "Do you want me to return your lunch tray for you?"

"Oh, no, thanks," Abby said, and then froze.

Brianna had appeared right beside them. She had a curious look on her face. "Did you say 'detention'?"

"I-I-I was saying, um, what a shame it is that kids get detention," Abby stammered. "It's, uh, really unfair."

Brianna's eyes opened wide. "Abby Hayes, did *you* get detention?"

"I'm not in trouble," Abby lied.

"Then why are you carrying your lunch tray out of the principal's office?"

"Brianna, don't you have a play to star in or something?" Mason asked. "Aren't the bright lights of Broadway waiting for you?"

Brianna smiled flirtatiously. "Of course they are, Mason. But I have time for my friends, too."

Abby groaned. She and Brianna hadn't been friends since kindergarten. Their friendship had lasted for about five minutes — until Brianna bragged that her pink sneakers were more expensive than Abby's, and that she acted in cereal commercials and had danced with a stuffed brontosaurus on TV.

"Is this why you aren't selling cookies in the school yard anymore, Abby?" Brianna patted her tiny waist. "Even though they were delicious, I'm glad. Last week I gained three ounces."

"You've got it all wrong," Abby began.

"I checked three times," Brianna said. "The scale never lies."

"Brianna . . ."

"I do understand." Brianna bestowed her most dazzling smile on Abby. "So sorry for your misfortune. This kind of thing goes on your permanent record, you know."

"Bug off, Brianna," Mason said.

"Don't worry, I won't tell anyone," Brianna promised. "I mean, I'll try not to." With a wave of her perfect, manicured hand, she disappeared down the hallway.

Chapter 13

Thursday

"O what a tangled web we weave,/When first we practise to deceive!"

—Sir Walter Scott

The Politician's Calendar

My sister Isabel has the annoying habit of reciting this whenever anyone in the Hayes family tells a lie or an untruth. And now it's been going through my head all day.

Even though she promised not to say anything, Brianna must have told someone, or at least dropped a hint. I've been found out by two of my best friends!

<u>Lies, Lies</u>

1. Hannah found out that I had lied by omission. (That means leaving things out.) I

didn't tell her what happened, and now she's upset and angry.

I said I was sorry, but Hannah says that she doesn't trust me anymore.

2. Sophia found out that there wasn't really a literary magazine project during lunch hour.

I said I was sorry, but Sophia is still hurt. She barely spoke to me in art class today.

What a mess!!!! Two of my best friends are furious, not because I was in trouble, but because I covered it up.

It would have been easier to tell the truth in the first place. But how was I supposed to know that?

Fortunately, all is not lost.

Things to Be Thankful For
Most people still don't know about my detention with Dr. Trane. (Thank you, Brianna.)

Most people also don't know that
I've been ordered to stop selling cookies for-
ever.
   So far most of the sixth grade hasn't
found out.
   So far Simon hasn't found out.
   So far no one on the literary journal has
found out.
   So far my family hasn't found out.

   Things could definitely be much worse.
(But I hope Hannah and Sophia forgive me
soon.)

On Thursday afternoon after school, Abby headed
straight up the stairs to her father's attic office. In
one hand, she had a folded piece of paper, and in the
other, she was carrying her backpack. She hesitated
for a moment before his closed office door, then
knocked and walked in.
   Her father's office was a cheerful, slightly messy
space. It was big and quiet, with skylights and thick
carpets. Books were stacked in piles on the floor, and
there were plants under the skylights.

"Hi, Dad, I'm home," she announced. "And I've got a permission slip for you to sign."

"Abby," her father said, "I'm glad to see you. Put the paper on my desk." He was typing rapidly at the computer. "I'll look at it later."

"I need you to sign it right away," she explained. "Otherwise I won't be able to watch the movie in social studies tomorrow."

Her father swiveled around in his chair and picked up the paper. He scanned it quickly and then scrawled his signature on the bottom.

"Thanks." Abby put it into her backpack and turned to leave. "You can go back to your work now."

"Don't be in such a hurry to go," her father said. "Sit down and let's talk. I only need to finish this e-mail."

Abby sat down on the couch. Then she leaned her head against a pillow and breathed a sigh of relief.

The office was peaceful. It felt good to sit there. It was good to be home, where nobody knew what had happened and where she didn't have to make up lies or excuses or apologize for having made them.

Her father clicked the send button. "Done!" he

said, turning around to face his daughter. "How was your day?"

"Fine," Abby said. If she forgot lunch with Dr. Trane and the fact that two of her closest friends were furious with her, as well as crossed off the continual worry she had that the rest of the sixth grade would find out about her detention, her day *had* been fine.

Paul Hayes opened a desk drawer, took a chocolate bar from his stash, and offered it to Abby.

Her father watched her devour the chocolate. "Hungry?"

"No," Abby lied.

"How many cookies did you sell today?"

She shrugged. "None."

"You've reached your goal already?"

"I'm, uh, taking a break for a while."

Her father looked at her steadily. "Is everything okay?"

"Of course!"

He picked up an envelope. "I got a letter from your principal today."

Abby's heart began to beat wildly.

"It's a notice of disciplinary action. I hear you've had lunch detention for the past week."

"Um, uh . . . really?"

Her father's eyes bored into hers. "Why didn't you tell us, Abby?"

Why? she thought. Because no one else in the Hayes family ever got in real trouble. But she couldn't say that to her father.

"I don't know," she mumbled.

"That's not an answer."

She hung her head. This was almost worse than being called to the principal's office.

"Dr. Trane says that you deliberately broke the rules," her father said. "This doesn't sound like you, Abby. What happened?"

"They wouldn't let me sell cookies in school," Abby began. "How else was I supposed to earn money for my writing program?"

"You should have come to us for help," her father said.

"I *did*," Abby retorted.

Her father was silent for a moment. Then he said, "That's not an excuse to deliberately break the rules."

"How do you expect me to obey the rules when I have to earn six hundred dollars?" Abby cried. "Isabel and Eva don't have to do *anything*! And they get to go to Europe! It's so unfair!"

"Sometimes life is like that," her father said. "One day you'll get your turn and Alex will say it's not fair."

"But what am I supposed to do *now*?" Abby retorted. "I don't care about the future. I just want to get into that writing program."

"Six hundred dollars *is* a lot of money for a sixth-grader to earn," her father admitted. "How much money do you still need?"

"About a hundred and fifty dollars."

"That's all? You're almost there," her father said. "Congratulations."

"For *what*? Forgetting lunch detention? For being the first person in the Hayes family to get sent to the principal's office?" Abby said. She felt on the verge of tears.

"*I've* gotten into trouble."

"Not you, Dad!"

"Once I climbed onto my high school roof and partied with friends during a high school assembly," her father confessed. "I got suspended for three days."

Abby stared at her father. "No way!"

"It's the truth," her father said, holding his hand up. "I know what it's like to get sent to the principal's office."

"But no one else in this family does," Abby insisted. "Can you imagine what Isabel and Eva are going to say?"

"You might be surprised," he said. "After all, if you can't be honest with your family, who can you talk to?"

"Don't tell them," Abby said. *"Please."* To her dismay, she began to cry.

"I won't tell anyone unless you say it's okay."

Abby reached for a tissue and blew her nose noisily. "Good."

"We're all proud of you," her father said quietly.

Abby stared at him in disbelief.

"I hope you'll come to us next time you're in trouble," he concluded. "You'll find us more understanding than you think."

"There won't be any next time!" Abby cried. She stood up and picked up her backpack.

After tomorrow, she was a new person. Not many people knew about her detention. She would put it behind her and move on with her life.

Chapter 14

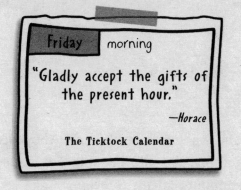

Friday morning

"Gladly accept the gifts of the present hour."
—Horace

The Ticktock Calendar

<u>Gifts of the Present Hour</u>

1. Last day of detention with Dr. Tranel! HOORAY!

2. Hannah called me last night. She said that in my place, she might have lied, too. (Except that she hates to lie, and so she probably wouldn't have.) But she could sort of see my point of view. She almost understood why I didn't tell her. So she's not as mad anymore. HOORAY!

3. My father isn't going to tell anyone in my family what happened. HOORAY!

4. After today, no one except Hannah,

Sophia, my father, and a very few others will ever know that I was in trouble. HOORAY!!

Oh, yeah, Brianna. She's forgotten me already. HOORAY!!!

Smiling and waving to her friends, Abby rushed into homeroom. She slid into her seat and waited for the morning announcements to begin.

One last lunch with Dr. Trane, Abby thought for the millionth time. And then she would tell her cookie customers that she wasn't baking anymore. Her father had given her an easy out.

"You can say that your parents won't let you," he said. "You can say that we think your homework is suffering. We'll take the blame."

As for the rest of the money she needed to earn for the writing program, he had promised to help her find a solution.

Abby felt as if a huge weight had been lifted from her shoulders. All in all, this was going to be a wonderful day.

Kids hurried in before the final bell rang. The

teacher began to take attendance. The clock ticked above the chalkboard.

"Good morning, middle-schoolers," came the too-cheerful voice of the school secretary from the speaker mounted on the wall. "Rise and shine. Swim team practice Saturday morning at five thirty A.M. in the freezing waters of the high school pool. Bring your soda can tabs to the art room by Friday. Happy birthday to our favorite Latin teacher, Mr. Cesare. . . ."

Abby's mind drifted off. She wondered what the last day of detention would be like. Would they have to eat in silence as usual? Would Dr. Trane say something encouraging to them, like, "You've done your time. Now let's forget this happened and make a new start."?

She hoped the pimply kid would have the sense to keep quiet.

"There'll be a meeting of the Comic Book Club today after school in room two seventeen. New members are welcome," the secretary continued. "And now, a special announcement from the principal's office. Dr. Trane?"

Abby sat up, suddenly attentive.

The principal cleared his throat. "This week I

found an individual selling food items in the school yard. This is a violation of school rules. The individual in question had her product confiscated and was put on detention. Next time I see any activity like this, that individual will be suspended."

All Abby's classmates turned to look at her. She slid down in her seat, wishing she could disappear.

"To repeat," Dr. Trane said, as if he hadn't said it clearly enough already, "it's a serious violation of the rules to sell cookies on school property."

Abby's face was burning. There was no question who he was talking about. Dr. Trane couldn't have made it any clearer if he had announced her name, the color of her hair, and her birth date. *Every single person* in Susan B. Anthony Middle School now knew that Abby Hayes was in deep trouble.

Chapter 15

Friday

"If you can't stand
the heat, get out of
the kitchen."

Grilling Calendar

I wish that I had never gone into the kitchen.

I wish that I had never baked the cookies.

I wish that I had never brought them to <u>The Daisy</u> meeting.

I wish that I had never sold them to my schoolmates.

I wish that my parents had enough money to send me to the writing program this year.

I wish that I hadn't decided to earn the money myself.

I wish that I hadn't started a business.

I wish that Dr. Trane hadn't caught me.

I wish that he had never given me lunch detention.

I wish that he hadn't made a public announcement.

I wish that the intercom speakers had all been turned off.

I wish that he hadn't mentioned the word "cookie" and tipped off the entire school as to my identity.

I was trying to get out of the kitchen, but IT'S TOO LATE!!!! I'm in the fire!!

With her arms hunched defensively around her books and her head down, Abby scurried to her next class.

If only she had known that Dr. Trane was going to make that announcement, she would have brought a disguise to school. Dark glasses and maybe a mustache. And definitely a wig. Her red hair was like a strobe light. People could pick her out from half a mile away.

Kids kept grabbing her arm and making obvious comments, like, "You're in hot water now!" or "You got sent to the principal's office!"

Well, *duh*.

Other kids seemed shocked. "Did you *know* that it was against the rules?" Or "I can't believe *you* did that, Abby Hayes!"

They looked at her as if she were some kind of criminal.

Then there was Lucas. "It's an outrage!" he cried. "I'm going to circulate a petition! Free the cookies! Cookies for the people!"

That was the last thing she needed.

Trying to get away from Lucas, Abby bumped into Natalie, who muttered something sympathetic, like, "Too bad. But it will pass."

When? Abby wondered. She hoped this would all blow over soon, even though she doubted it.

"Way to go!" yelled a kid who had been suspended from school earlier that year. "I didn't know you had it in you."

What did she have in her? Sneaky thoughts? Cookies?

Too many lunches eaten under the eye of Dr. Trane?

And then Abby saw Simon. He shook his head, seemed about to say something, then walked on.

Feeling as if she had just run the gauntlet, Abby sighed with relief as she hurried through the door to her next class.

There was silence as she took her seat. Everyone turned to look at her.

Next to her, Bethany shook her head sorrowfully. "I didn't think you were that kind of person, Abby."

"I'm not," Abby said. Did breaking one rule turn her into a totally different person? She was still Abby. Who did everyone think she was?

Chapter 16

Saturday

"The cat is out of the bag."

The Fairy Tale Calendar

A hundred cats are out of a hundred bags. That's what it feels like.

My teachers know.
My friends know.
My enemies know.
My cookie customers know.
My crush knows.
The janitor knows.
The school nurse and the librarian know.
Probably the school bus drivers know, too.

Even my sisters and brother know now.
Last night, I came home and told them.

Eva said, "I can't believe you went ahead and broke a school rule."
Isabel said, "You weren't afraid of getting in trouble?"
And Alex just stared at me with big eyes. Like he didn't know what unexpected thing I was going to do next.

My siblings seemed so shocked, I was embarrassed and uncomfortable. But I'm glad I told them.

There's a certain relief in having everything out in the open.
Like, I don't have to lie anymore. And I don't have to worry about being found out, either. There's nothing more to fear. I made a huge mistake in front of the whole world, but I lived to tell the tale.

I feel a strange sense of relaxation. This is all over. It really IS all over. I don't even have to worry about money anymore. When I counted up what I had, I discovered I was only one hundred thirty-eight dollars short. Dad agreed to give me the money, if I washed his car for him every other weekend for the next three months.

This afternoon I watched old comedies with Hannah. We made huge bowls of popcorn. We sat around laughing and eating and occasionally throwing popcorn at each other.

Then Hannah went home and I went upstairs to write in my journal.

Even though I never want to hear the C-word again, I can't stop thinking about how it all happened.

Oddest Thing
Baking one batch of cookies for the literary journal led to a cookie empire.

Most Unexpected Thing
My baking talent. Discovering a chocolate thumb!

Worst Thing
Lunch detention with Dr. Trane.

Most Embarrassing Thing
Dr. Trane's public announcement. Finding myself the topic of schoolwide gossip. Having everyone know that I was in trouble.

Funniest Thing
That pimply kid calling the principal Choo-Choo Trane. I can't get it out of my head.

Stupidest Thing
Telling all those lies, which got me into worse trouble.

Best Thing
I'm going to the writing program! All I have to do is wash Dad's car a bunch of times to earn the rest of the money.

Sweetest Thing

Mason helping me sell cookies every day, sharing detention with me, and never seeming to mind.

Craziest Thing

That pimply kid was willing to climb out the principal's window for only two dollars.

Happiest Thing

Hannah has almost forgiven me! (And Sophia is starting to talk to me again.)

Thing I Most Want to Remember

I felt like I was going to die when Dr. Trane caught us, and then again when he made that public announcement. But I didn't. I survived! It's okay to make mistakes sometimes. (But I hope I don't make another one like that anytime soon!)

Hooray! It's over! It's REALLY OVER!!

And a few more miscellaneous surprises.

Eva just came into my room while I was
writing this.

"Don't ever tell anyone what I'm about
to tell you," she whispered.

"Okay, sure," I said.

"I know you're embarrassed about getting
in trouble." My sister leaned close. "I got
sent to the principal's office in eighth
grade," she confessed.

"Who, _you_?"

"I used Magic Marker to write the name
of my crush all over the girls' bathroom,"
she said. "Someone saw me and turned me
in. The principal was going to call Mom and
Dad, but I offered to clean it up instead."

"Wow," I breathed.

"No one knows," Eva said sternly. "Not
even Isabel. So don't tell her."

"I won't," I whispered.

No sooner had she left than Isabel appeared.

Like Eva, she was holding a finger to her
lips. "I know it was really hard for you to

get sent to the principal's office, Abby," she whispered.

"Yeah."

"I feel your pain," Isabel said. "Once I got in trouble, just like you."

"For baking cookies?"

"For yelling at a teacher."

I gasped. "Why?"

"Because he had his facts wrong and wouldn't admit it," Isabel snapped. "I lost my temper and let him have it. He sent me to the principal's office. I got off with a warning."

She lowered her voice. "No one knows. Not even Eva. Keep it secret."

"I won't tell," I promised.

I think someone slipped truth serum into the macaroni and cheese.

Alex just came into my room and confessed that once he planted a robot in his teacher's purse.

"She knew it was me," Alex said. "I don't know how."

My father already told me about his rooftop party. But I didn't know that he skipped school with half a dozen of his friends and got picked up by the police in a state park.

And my mother tiptoed into my room, too. My father had told her a few days ago. She didn't say anything to me. Until today.

"Don't tell anyone," she began.

I stared. "You, too, Mom?"

She looked embarrassed. "It was just a stupid prank," she said. "When I was a senior in high school, my friends and I toilet-papered the principal's car."

"That's awesome."

My mother gave me a look. "Don't even think about it."

"I won't," I promised.

"Dr. Trane is too scary."

Okay. Forget about what I wrote about my family being so perfect.

I guess they aren't.

I guess they DO know what it's like to get in trouble.

But why did they wait so long to tell me?

And why does everyone tell me to keep it a secret?

What's the big deal?

Why are they all so embarrassed?

I know! The Hayes family needs a special holiday!

I hereby declare tomorrow <u>Embarrassment-free Day</u>!

We'll spill our secrets, have a mischief competition, and give out a Don't Be So Perfect Award. The person who can relate the most awful incident will get lunch detention with Dr. Trane for a month.

Ha-ha, just kidding.

The grand prize will be a dozen chocolate chip cookies.

Store-bought, OF COURSE!!!

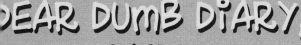

SPEND YOUR DAY THE ABBY WAY!

The Amazing Days of Abby Hayes® by Anne Mazer

In a family of superstars, it's hard to stand out. But Abby is about to surprise her friends, her family, and most of all, herself!

Hang out with Abby at
www.scholastic.com/abbyhayes

Have you read them all?

❏	0-439-14977-0	#1 Every Cloud Has a Silver Lining	$4.99
❏	0-439-17876-2	#2 The Declaration of Independence	$4.99
❏	0-439-17877-0	#3 Reach for the Stars	$4.99
❏	0-439-17878-9	#4 Have Wheels, Will Travel	$4.99
❏	0-439-17881-9	#5 Look Before You Leap	$4.99
❏	0-439-17882-7	#6 The Pen Is Mightier Than the Sword	$4.99
❏	0-439-35366-1	#7 Two Heads Are Better Than One	$4.99
❏	0-439-35367-X	#8 The More, the Merrier	$4.99
❏	0-439-35368-8	#9 Out of Sight, Out of Mind	$4.99
❏	0-439-35369-6	#10 Everything New Under the Sun	$4.99
❏	0-439-48273-9	#11 Too Close for Comfort	$4.99
❏	0-439-48280-1	#12 Good Things Come in Small Packages	$4.99
❏	0-439-48281-X	#13 Some Things Never Change	$4.99
❏	0-439-48282-8	Super Special #1 The Best Is Yet to Come	$5.99
❏	0-439-63775-9	Super Special #2 Knowledge Is Power	$5.99
❏	0-439-68063-8	#14 It's Music to My Ears	$4.99
❏	0-439-68066-2	#15 Now You See It, Now You Don't	$4.99
❏	0-439-68067-0	#16 That's the Way the Cookie Crumbles	$4.99

■SCHOLASTIC

ABB11